For Szymon,

Go for Gold!

First published in Great Britain in 2011 by Simon and Schuster UK Ltd,
a CBS company.

Simon & Schuster UK Ltd
1st Floor, 222 Gray's Inn Road, London WC1X 8HB

A CIP catalogue record for this book is available from the British Library.

978-1-84738-729-5

3 5 7 9 10 8 6 4 2

Printed and bound in Great Britain.

www.simonandschuster.co.uk

www.tamsynmurray.co.uk

STUNT BUNNY
RABBIT RACER
SB RACING
SB
FINISH
NISH
FINISH
FINISH
SB RACING
SB RACING
109
TAMSYN MURRAY
ILLUSTRATED BY LEE WILDISH

For Taz, my oldest four-legged friend.

Purr on, baby!

CHAPTER ONE

The New Neighbour

Let me introduce myself. I'm Harriet Houdini – Stunt Bunny extraordinaire and all-round superstar. Once upon a time, I was an ordinary little rabbit in an ordinary little pet shop, but then eight–year-old Susie Wilson took me home and my life changed for ever.

Before I knew it, I'd scooped first prize in the *Superpets Search for a Superstar* TV talent show and triple backflipped my way into the nation's hearts. Suddenly, I was a VIP – Very Important Pet – and everyone knew my name.

Of course, you might think that being the star of Saturday night television means I'm one of those snobby celebs who owns a big mansion with twenty-four-hour security guards, but you'd be wrong. I live with the Wilson family, in a normal-sized house on a perfectly everyday street. OK, so maybe my hutch is a teensy bit posh, but I am Britain's Best Loved Bunny, after all.

But when our new next-door neighbour moved in, our street became a little bit less ordinary. From the moment the mysterious Madame Belladonna arrived and fired a toothy smile my way, I had a peculiar, can't-quite-put-your-finger-on-it suspicion that there was something fishy about her. You might think I'm being twitchy, but after two bunny-napping attempts by a mad magician called the Great Maldini, a girl can't be too careful. He'd been after me ever since I won the village pet show and started on my rollercoaster ride to fame, but I wasn't about to spend the rest of my days popping in and out of an old

top hat in his rubbishy magic show. Luckily my Stunt Bunny skills had helped me escape his clutches both times.

But, even though I know I can be a bit suspicious, I still had a very funny feeling when our new neighbour arrived. I was sipping on a carrot smoothie while Susie read me some fan mail when I noticed a battered blue-and-green van pull up at the empty house next door. Susie had heard the noise too, so she lifted me up and carried me to the window so we could take a closer look.

'It looks like someone is moving in next door, Harriet,' she said, peering

through the net curtains. 'I wonder if they've got any pets?'

'Huh,' said Susie's dad as he came into the room. 'I hope not. One rabbit on the rampage is enough.'

Susie's dad is the grumpiest person I've ever met. I call him Evil Edward, or EE for short. He doesn't like me much and acts as though I'm always up to no good – even when I'm mostly behaving myself. He's especially suspicious where his precious garden is concerned, but it's his own fault really; if he didn't grow the most delicious roses, I wouldn't need to nibble them.

Susie's mum and little sister, Lily,

crowded around the window too, while the family cat, Smudge, jumped on to the window sill to see what all the fuss was about. We all watched as the new neighbour got out of the van.

'Oh, it's an old lady,' Susie said, sounding a little bit disappointed.

'What an odd-looking person,' Mrs Wilson said, peering at the new neighbour uncertainly. 'Is that a beekeeper's hat she's wearing?'

Sure enough, the old lady was wearing a big, broad-brimmed hat with a thick veil all the way around it. The rest of her appearance was just as strange: her dress was purple and flowery and didn't quite fit her thin body, and sticking out of her pointy, high-heeled shoes was a pair of skinny, hairy legs. She was carrying a gigantic, empty birdcage. Smudge licked his lips and

his tail began to swish from side to side.

'Gosh,' EE said as the lady tottered past our window towards the path to her front door. 'I hope she doesn't have a parrot to live in that cage. I don't want to hear it screeching "Pretty Polly" at all hours of the day and night.'

Lily took her dolly out of her mouth. 'Pretty Polly, Pretty Polly,' she squawked.

'Me and my big mouth,' EE sighed, folding his arms. 'I suppose we'd better go and say hello.' Then he looked down at me, a stern look on his face. 'Leave that rabbit in here, Susie, we don't want to scare the poor woman away.'

Huh, what on earth was he going on

about? If anyone was going to put our new neighbour off, it was him!

Susie frowned. ‘Harriet wants to say hello too.’

EE made a tutting sound. ‘Oh, all right, but make sure she can’t escape.’

‘I’m sure she’ll be on her best behaviour,’ Susie said, clipping me into my sparkly silver harness and lead. Then we opened the front door to greet the new arrival.

‘‘Hello,’ EE called out. ‘Welcome to the neighbourhood. We’re the Wilsons.’ The old lady didn’t stop, but waved a woolly-gloved hand and carried on wobbling her way along the path.

'Do let us know if you need anything,' Mrs Wilson added, her big, friendly smile fading a little.

The woman reached her front door. ''Ow lovely to meet you, my dears,' she said in a squeaky, accented voice. 'My name ees Madame Belladonna. I am sure we will be – 'ow you say – ze best bunnies.'

'I think you mean best buddies,' EE corrected with a chuckle.

The veiled hat nodded up and down. 'Zat ees what I say.' Balancing the birdcage on one hand, she opened her front door and turned around to stare at me. 'She ees ze cutest leetle rabbit, no? I look forward to getting to know 'er much better.'

The door closed, leaving the Wilsons staring at each other and me frowning suspiciously. There was something weird about Madame Belladonna and I didn't just mean her clothes. I wasn't sure I wanted to get to know her at all.

'Well, she seemed . . . nice,' Mrs Wilson

said as we trooped back into our own house.

'Hmmm,' EE said. 'She's a few bees short of a hive if you ask me.'

I could hardly concentrate on my fan mail after that. Something about our new neighbour bothered me, but I couldn't work out what it was. One thing I did know: I'd be keeping a very close eye on Madame Belladonna. She looked like a crazy customer.

CHAPTER TWO

Tornado Taz Twists Into Town

I try hard to be a friendly rabbit – a real you-tickle-my-tummy-and-I'll-tickle-yours type. So when the director of *Superpets*, glamorous Gloria Goodwood, announced that there was going to be a new pet joining our one-off, *Summer Special* show, my ears pricked up

straight away. People kept all kinds of unusual animals. The new addition might be a jellyfish who juggled or a piano-playing pig. But whether they were cuddly or clammy, I really hoped we'd get along.

And, even better, Gloria told us that some of the pets who had been on the *Superpets Live* tour were now going to join the main cast of *Superpets* too. So not only might I make a new friend, I'd also be seeing my old ones too!

To be honest, though, I was a bit disappointed when I first saw the new pet. Tornado Taz looked like an ordinary, everyday cat, the kind

you might see eying up the birds in next-door's garden. But his tabby stripes hid a terrific talent, as I found out when I hopped over to say hello.

'He might not look much now,' Taz's owner, Tim, was saying to the make-up lady, 'but wait until he gets on to the obstacle course. You won't see him for dust.'

'Obstacle course?' said the make-up lady, gazing down at the cat in confusion. 'You mean jumps and tunnels and weaving in and out of poles? Like dogs do?'

Tim pushed his glasses up and beamed with pride. 'Exactly right.

Taz is the world's first agility cat!'

I stared at Taz, who was perched on the make-up chair. He threw me an embarrassed look which said, 'Owners – don't you just love 'em?'

Then Gloria appeared. 'It's time for your screen test, Taz. Let's see if the camera loves you the way it loves Harriet here.'

She led Taz and his owner across the studio floor to a series of obstacles. Susie and I followed, settling down next to the cameraman to watch. This was going to be interesting.

I wasn't the only one who wanted to see what Taz was made of. I spotted

Lulu the chimpanzee lowering her hula hoop and Spike-tacular, the hedgehog dance troupe, piling on top of each other for a better view. Everyone held their breath as Taz padded up to the start line and crouched down, his tail sticking straight out behind him and his ears laid flat against his head.

Gloria held up her hand. 'On your marks . . . get set . . . go!'

Before you could say 'super speedy', Taz was off, streaking towards the first jump so fast that his stripes became just a blur. He cleared the sticks with ease and shot like a bullet through a long, black cloth tunnel. Then he was weaving in and out of a set of tall red-and-white poles and over another jump, before zooming up a thin plank of wood to a balancing bar high above the ground.

Next to me, Cherry the counting kitten lost track of the number of obstacles and covered her eyes with

her paws. Even Spike-tacular, who do some pretty acrobatic dance moves, looked nervous. But Taz was a cool cat. He was across the bar and down the other side without even a hint of a wobble. As he raced over the finish line, Gloria clicked the stopwatch in her hand and smiled.

'Less than one minute,' she said to Tim. 'I can see why you call him Tornado Taz. Our viewers are going to love him!'

'I don't call that much of a talent,' a voice behind me drawled. I didn't need to turn around to know it belonged to Miranda, the snooty owner of Doodle the opera-singing Poodle. The only bad

thing about the *Superpets Live* pets joining the cast was that Miranda and Doodle were now on the show too. We'd been enemies ever since I won *Superpets Search for a Superstar* instead of Doodle and the two of them were always on the lookout for ways to cause me trouble. They'd sunk to new dastardly lows while we were on tour and I suspected they'd even been in cahoots with the Great Maldini, but I'd outsmarted them all. Today, though, their attention was fixed on Taz.

'Surely any animal could jump over a few sticks and run along a pole,' Miranda went on, looking down her

nose at Gloria fussing over Tim and Taz. 'It's nowhere near as difficult as singing.'

Sam, the nine-year-old owner of Spike-tacular, sniggered. 'If you call what Doodle does singing.'

Miranda scowled at him. 'Opera is very hard to perform, I'll have you know. Doodle is the most talented pet this show has ever seen.'

Gloria came towards us. 'It's funny you should say that, Miranda. I don't want any one-trick ponies on my show so I've decided that, apart from Taz, each pet has to learn a new talent, which they'll perform on the live *Summer Special*. With all the new

animals joining the show we need to have a real shake-up. So anyone who doesn't knock my socks off . . .' She paused and looked around at us gravely. 'Well, let's just say they won't be part of the *Superpets* crew.'

Everyone looked suddenly nervous. Cherry stopped counting the number of pets crowded around Gloria. Spike-tacular froze mid-pyramid and I saw Trevor and his tumbling terrapins gulp anxiously.

'I'll be watching you all very closely over the next few weeks,' Gloria went on. 'I do hope none of you will be leaving *Superpets*.'

With one final glance around, she disappeared around the back of the camera. As the other animals and their owners wandered away, Susie reached down to give my grey fur a soothing rub. 'Don't worry, Harriet,' she whispered in an uncertain voice. 'I'm sure you'll be OK.'

EE appeared next to us, a cup of steaming coffee in his hand. 'Do you know, they have the most marvellous cakes in the studio canteen?' He patted his tummy in satisfaction. 'I could have

stayed there all afternoon.'

Then he noticed Susie's worried face. 'What's wrong?'

'Gloria just announced that all the pets have to find a new talent,' Susie said, her bottom lip wobbling like jelly. 'Or they'll have to leave *Superpets*.'

EE frowned. 'If anyone has to go, it should be that silly poodle and her owner. She could sour milk with that voice and that doesn't count as a talent.'

Susie's blue eyes swam with tears. 'But what if it's Harriet? She's only ever done bunny backflips. What if that's all she can do?'

EE put his arm around her. 'Don't tell anyone I said this, but Harriet's got star quality. I'm sure she'll come up with something fresh to impress Gloria.'

Any other time, I would have been amazed to hear EE say something nice about me, but I was distracted by Miranda and Doodle huddling together

in a corner. Miranda whispered into the poodle's ear and then they both looked over at me and grinned unpleasantly. My whiskers twitched with anxiety. They were plotting one of their evil tricks, or my name wasn't Harriet Houdini. Watching them, I came to a fast decision; I'd show them exactly what a show-stopping performance was made of. And this time, there'd be no more Miss Nice Bunny.

CHAPTER THREE

George's Giggling Guinea Pigs

Our neighbours at number fifty-three were Mr and Mrs Green and their son, George. For as long as I could remember, George had been on the lookout for the perfect pet. He'd tried several, including a goldfish who'd accidentally been flushed down the loo, a hamster

who sneaked into his rucksack and got lost at school, and a budgie which had flown out of an open window when Mrs Green was cleaning out its cage.

So, when Susie told me that George had bought a pair of guinea pigs, Salt and Pepper, I was curious to see how long they would stick around. Then the Greens went on holiday and the guinea pigs moved into our garden for a couple of weeks. Suddenly, the chances of an escape attempt went through the roof. For one thing Susie's little sister loved anything furry and there was no way she'd be able to resist the guinea pigs. Once she'd smuggled them up to her bedroom to play with her dollies, they'd be goners for sure. And if Lily didn't get them, Smudge would. I'd already spotted him sitting on top of their cage, staring downwards in a hungry way.

Ever since Gloria had told us the least-talented animals would be leaving *Superpets*, I'd been thinking like crazy about my new trick and had tried backflipping on to anything bouncy I found lying about in the garden. My favourite was Susie's red-and-yellow striped beach-ball. I wasn't so keen on EE's deckchair, especially after I'd accidentally boinged off his tummy

when I'd forgotten he was there. I kept up the hard work, though. I wasn't ready to give up my position as Britain's Number One Bunny, no matter what Doodle and Miranda had planned.

But Salt and Pepper weren't exactly quiet guests. EE had put their cage facing mine and every time I practised a bounce, the two of them let out a chattering 'meep' noise that sounded like they were giggling their heads off. It drove me mad and I wasn't the only person they were getting to.

‘What is that noise?’ EE said, one Sunday afternoon when Susie was sitting in the garden watching me hop around the flowerbeds. He lifted the newspaper from over his face and glared around. ‘Can’t a man rest his eyes in the sunshine without a racket breaking out?’

Of course, Salt and Pepper thought this was hilarious as well and their giggling got louder.

EE scowled. 'Shut them up, please,' he groaned at Mrs Wilson. 'I'm trying to read the paper.'

She carried on hanging out the washing. 'Mrs Green did say they were quite high-spirited,' she said. 'I'm sure they'll settle down in a minute.'

I was just hopping nearer to the rose bushes, wondering if I could use the distraction to chomp a petal or two, when I caught a movement in Madame Belladonna's garden. Looking over, I blinked. Hovering above the top of the fence was a gigantic pink pom-pom. Smudge spotted it too. He watched it for a moment and then leaped up on to

the fence and sank his claws into the pom-pom.

There was a high-pitched yelp and Smudge let go. He jumped down from the fence and hid behind EE's leg, hissing. On the other side of the fence, Madame Belladonna shot upwards.

We all stared. Even though it was a warm and sunny afternoon, Madame Belladonna had a yellow scarf wrapped around her neck right up to her nose and she was wearing a pair of swimming goggles. The pink pom-pom that Smudge had attacked was attached to a woolly, lime-green hat.

'Lost something, Madame Belladonna?' EE called.

'Signor Wilson, you give me ze frights,' she said, in her funny voice. ''Ere I am, looking for . . . ze chicken eggs and zat pussy cat attacks me like I was ze mouse.'

EE looked puzzled. 'I didn't know you had chickens over there?'

Madame Belladonna let out a loud squawking laugh, which set the guinea pigs off giggling too. 'Zere are no chickens 'ere? Zat ees why I do not find ze eggs. Seelly me!' And throwing a final beady-eyed look my way from behind her goggles, she tottered back up the garden and disappeared into her house.

EE and Mrs Wilson watched her go, confused looks on their faces.

'You know, I think she might be a little bit loopy,' EE said, shaking his head in pity.

'She's certainly got unusual dress sense," Mrs Wilson agreed. 'Maybe she's

just misunderstood. It might help if we got to know her better.'

EE looked doubtful. 'I don't see how. But I suppose I could get her a ticket for the *Superpets Summer Special*. When she finds out she's living next door to some VIPs, she might get a bit star-struck and behave herself.'

Well, if that wasn't just like EE, basking in the spotlight of my talent! I snuggled up to Susie and hoped he'd forget about that ridiculous idea. What with Salt and Pepper one side and Madame Belladonna the other, things were getting crazy in the Wilson house, and I didn't really want our

nutty neighbour turning up at the *Superpets* studio. The way things were shaping up, it was the only place I could go for a bit of peace and quiet.

CHAPTER FOUR

Doodle's Dastardly Deed

There are two types of star on *Superpets:* those who understand how lucky they are to be part of the show, and the ones who think no one would watch if it wasn't for them. I'm in the first group. I love the smell of the make-up and the roar of the audience

and can't wait to get out there and entertain people. But as you might guess, Doodle isn't. She thinks she's the bee's knees and Miranda agrees with her. The list of demands they made when we were on tour was amazing and changed all the time.

'Doodle needs fresh spring water from the Welsh mountains and a cashmere rug in her dressing room,' Miranda declared, as we waited backstage on Saturday for the rehearsal to start. 'She can't be expected to hit the high notes if she's forced to drink common tap water and lie on a dirty rug.'

Gloria gave a brisk smile and winked

at me and Susie on her way past. 'I expect Doodle will need even more luxuries for her new trick, won't she, Miranda?'

Miranda and Doodle stared at each other. 'Oh – er – of course!' Miranda trilled. 'She's been working terribly hard.'

Tim nudged EE. 'I bet a talented bunny like Harriet has a long list of things she needs to pull off her amazing stunts.'

EE chewed on the chocolate bar he'd picked up at the snack machine and looked down at me. 'She's watching her weight. An organic carrot before she goes on stage, and that's about it.'

I wiggled my ears in outrage; me, watching my weight? If anyone needed to go on a diet around here, it was EE. His tummy was getting so big he could hardly see his toes.

Tim nodded. 'Taz is the same. He's an athlete.'

Taz let out a hungry miaow and eyed EE's chocolate bar.

'In fact,' Tim went on, ignoring the cat, 'I think there might be a touch of cheetah in his ancestry. He's always been fast and I'm sure he has a few black spots in amongst his tabby stripes.'

We all peered at Taz's sleek coat and he blinked in embarrassment at his

owner's boasting. I twitched my nose in sympathy. What can I say? Being famous isn't always fun.

'Look, Dad, Harriet and Taz are becoming friends,' Susie said, when she saw us looking at each other.

'Not for long,' a voice behind me mumbled. Peering through the bars

of my travel basket, I saw Miranda and Doodle smirking in my direction. I knew they were up to no good, but what were they planning?

'That cherry pie they're serving in the canteen is simply delicious,' Miranda said in a loud voice. 'Shame they were about to run out.'

EE pricked up his ears. 'Cherry pie, you say?' He looked at Tim. 'I don't know about you, but I could do with a little something to eat.

All this exercise makes me peckish.'

Tim hesitated. "Shouldn't we stay with the pets?"

Glancing around, EE shook his head. 'They'll be OK for a few minutes.'

Susie poked a finger into her dad's belly. 'Mum says you're not supposed to have cakes. She says if you get any fatter, you won't fit into your clothes.'

EE wiped the last crumbs of chocolate from around his mouth. 'No one said anything about cake. It's pie we're going to have. Come on, Tim, let's get down there before it's too late.'

Tim reached down to tickle Taz behind the ears. 'Back in a minute, Puss.'

Susie watched their retreating backs for a moment, then wagged a finger in front of my basket. 'Wait here, Harriet. I better keep an eye on him.' She followed EE and Tim and her voice faded into the distance. 'I'm going to tell Mum about this . . .'

And then we were on our own. Behind us, I could practically feel Miranda grinning.

'Poor Harriet, all locked away,' I heard her say. 'Wouldn't you like to stretch your legs?'

She reached down and unclipped the

locks on my basket. The door swung open. Suspiciously, I poked my velvet nose out. Miranda wasn't known for her kind deeds. Why was she letting me out?

I glanced over at Taz. Miranda was undoing the leather straps on his basket and tugging the door open for him as well. But Taz was new to *Superpets* and a lot more trusting than me. Purring gratefully, he padded out of the basket and stretched.

'Would you like a snack, Harriet?' Miranda asked, waving a delicious-smelling carrot in front of me.

I couldn't help it; I hopped towards it, my mouth watering at the thought of sinking my teeth into its orangey goodness.

'Now, Doodle!' Miranda cried and everything seemed to happen at once.

Doodle let out a low growl and lunged towards Taz. With a terrified yowl, Taz sprang up in the air. I looked up to see him descending towards me, claws flashing in the lights. Thoughts of the tasty carrot flew out of my head. If I didn't get out of the way, I'd be in bunny bits before I could blink!

CHAPTER FIVE

Harriet Houdini: Rabbit Racer

I didn't fancy being a bunny pincushion, so quicker than you could say 'cutting claws' I jumped out of the way. Taz landed exactly where I'd been seconds before. Doodle snarled at the cat again and snapped her teeth at his tabby tail. Confused, Taz sped

towards me and I knew if I didn't move, there'd be a bumper bump. So I did the only thing I could. I ran.

We raced through the backstage area towards the studio stage, Doodle chasing Taz and Taz chasing me. The make-up lady dropped her powder puff, the cameraman leaped out of the way and Gloria looked flabbergasted as we flashed past. And before I knew what was happening we were on Taz's obstacle course!

'Harriet!' I heard Susie screech, but I didn't stop. Even though part of me knew that Taz wouldn't really hurt me, it felt like the call of the wild had taken over.

My rabbit ancestors were screaming at me to run from their ancient enemy, the cat.

Obstacles loomed in front of me. Without thinking, I somersaulted over the first jump and tore through the long cloth tunnel. Behind me, I heard a cheer and guessed Taz had cleared the jump too. Then I was on to the weaving poles. They quivered as I hopped madly from side to side.

Once I was through, I set my sights on the balancing bar up ahead. It wasn't until I heard the laughter that I slowed down and risked a glance over my shoulder.

Taz was skidding to a halt too. Straight away, I saw the reason for the laughter. Doodle had tried to follow us through the tunnel.

She must have realised far too late that her body was too big to fit through the plastic entrance and she was stuck with the tunnel flopping around her head like an elephant's trunk. It waggled from side to side as she tried to free herself and she let out a frightened whimper.

Miranda rushed on to the stage to free her. 'My poor Doody-Woody,' she squealed, pulling the tunnel off Doodle's face and staring into the dog's confused eyes anxiously. 'What have those nasty animals done to you?'

Taz and I exchanged looks. What had we done to Doodle? Surely it was more

a case of what the poodle had done to us?

Gloria bustled forward. 'Really, Miranda, you must learn to control that dog better. Or is Doodle in training to become a circus clown?'

A sulky pout crossed Miranda's face. 'Taz tried to scratch Doodle,' she said. 'I saw it with my own eyes. He should be thrown off the show.'

EE and Tim rushed over with Susie. She flung her arms around me in a big hug.

'Thrown off the show?' Tim repeated, rubbing Taz's ears and gazing around in bemusement. 'What's going on?'

'We were only gone a few minutes,' EE said, wiping what looked like cherry sauce from his chin. He eyed me in disbelief. 'That basket is supposed to be practically escape-proof. How did you get out this time, Harriet?'

'Come to think of it, how did Taz escape from his?' Tim wondered. 'I'm sure I locked him in.'

Everyone turned to look at Miranda.

'It wasn't anything to do with me,' she declared, folding her arms and glaring around. 'My poor Doodle is the victim here. Look, she's shaking.'

Doodle blinked and began to shiver. But Gloria was staring at the obstacle

course, a thoughtful expression on her face. 'This gives me an idea,' she said, tapping her lips with her finger. 'Harriet and Taz were super speedy. What if we put them head to head in a race, for the *Summer Special*?'

I thought about that. Racing over the obstacles had been fun, but was I faster than Taz? Casting a quick glance sideways, I wondered what he thought of the idea. His eyes gleamed and he swished his tail.

'Taz is up for it if Harriet is,' Tim said, looking enthusiastic. 'Kitty versus Bunny sounds good to me.'

Gloria smiled. 'And what about Harriet?' she asked, glancing between EE and Susie.

EE blushed, the way he always did when Gloria spoke to him. 'Nyurgh,' he mumbled. 'Whatever you say, G-G-Gloria.'

Susie looked at me and I waved my paws to let her know I was raring to race. 'I think that means she can't wait.'

'It looks as though you've found your new talent,' Gloria said, winking at me. 'From now on, you'll be Harriet Houdini – Rabbit Racer.'

I thumped the floor in excitement. Win or lose, this race was going to be FUN! And maybe I'd find a way to throw in some of my new tricks to make sure my place on *Superpets* was safe.

CHAPTER SIX

Things That Go Bump In The Night

Susie didn't waste any time once we got back home from the studio. Armed with a stopwatch and a clipboard, she put me straight into training. Round and round the garden I raced, while Susie marked down the times and Smudge watched with

a 'glad-it's-not-me' look on his face. I even got to use EE's beloved runner beans as weaving poles and there wasn't a thing he could do about it. The thunderous look on his face as the poles shuddered and shook was a picture.

'Careful!' he bellowed, as the young beans wobbled on their stalks above my head. 'They're not ready to be picked yet.'

They looked juicy enough to me, so it wouldn't be a bad thing if a few fell off while I was training . . . Next I hurtled through Susie's hula hoop and scooted up the bottom of

Lily's plastic yellow slide. As I raced through the skipping-rope finish line, Susie clicked the stopwatch and peered at the clipboard. 'That's great, Harriet. I'm sure you'll be faster than Taz.'

Salt and Pepper sat side by side in their hutch, watching me with bright, black eyes. I shook out my tail and hopped back to the start of the course. Susie might be confident I could win, but I wasn't so sure. Taz had been racing since he was a fluffy little kitten. He was a proper agility cat. If I wanted to beat him, I'd have to smash my best time and I didn't mind practising until my paws hurt to make that happen.

Susie didn't agree. 'That's enough for one day,' she said firmly, lifting me up and carrying me towards my hutch. 'It will be dark soon and you need a good night's sleep.'

Huh, I thought, there was no chance of that. Salt and Pepper were party animals who thought sleep was for wimps. I'd lost count of how many

times their noise had woken me from my dreams of Hollywood film premieres and gigantic crunchy carrots. Pet-sitting was hard work and I couldn't wait until the Greens got back from their holiday. I needed a rest!

I was snuggled up in the hay of my hutch when the first clatter woke me up. At first, I thought it was Salt and Pepper misbehaving, but then I heard a muffled moan and I frowned. That wasn't the gormless giggle of a guinea pig, it was more like the stifled yelp of someone stubbing their toe, and it sounded nearby. Instantly,

I was wide awake and hopping to the door of my hutch for a better look.

The trouble was, I couldn't see a thing. It was dark and, in spite of all the carrots I ate, I couldn't make out much in the moonlit garden. Then my eyes began to adjust and I saw two pairs of eyes glittering opposite me: Salt and Pepper. They too were crouched at the front of their hutch, noses pressed against the wire of the door. For once they were completely silent.

Suddenly, a movement caught my eye. Over by the fence, someone was coming our way. The only person I could think of who would wander around people's gardens in the middle of the night was a burglar, and that wasn't a cheery thought at all. The Wilsons would be tucked up in bed, fast asleep by now. Who was going to stop the shadowy figure from breaking into their house?

There was only one thing for it: I'd have to try and raise as much of a ruckus as possible. Hoping Salt and Pepper would get the idea and join in, I lifted up my back legs and fired them as hard as I could at the wall of my hutch. They connected with the wood with an enormous thud, which boomed across the still night air like cannon fire.

The guinea pigs meeped in shock and the figure leaped high into the air with a surprised shriek.

But a strange thing happened when the figure landed. Instead of hitting the floor and running away, like I expected, the burglar seemed to struggle to keep their balance. In fact, they began to career across the garden, waving their arms in the air and colliding with Mrs Wilson's washing, a big, white sheet wrapping itself around their head.

In a flash, I realised what had happened; Susie must have forgotten to put her roller skates away after playing with them today and the

burglar's feet had found them! Wrapping my ears around my head, I waited for the crash. It came seconds later. I peered out of my hutch.

Above the fence to Mr and Mrs Green's garden, a pair of upside-down legs waved in the moonlight and the sound of grunts and groans filled the air. The window over the kitchen flew

open and EE's grumpy voice rang out.

'What's going on out there?'

The legs froze. Then, with a final loud grunt, they disappeared into the Greens' garden. I heard a crashing noise and a howl of pain as the sheet-coated burglar bumped into Mrs Green's hanging baskets. After that everything went quiet. EE closed the bedroom window and the guinea pigs and I listened for signs that the burglar was coming back. There were none. I started to breathe more slowly. Whoever it was seemed to have gone.

Salt and Pepper celebrated the only way they knew how: noisily. Within seconds,

EE had flung open the window again.

'Will you animals be quiet down there? Some of us are trying to get some sleep!'

He had a cheek – how many times had Mrs Wilson moaned that his snoring was keeping her awake? Salt and Pepper must have thought the same because they ignored him completely, continuing with their inane chattering. Then a brilliant idea hit me. I rooted around in my hay for the carrot tops from my supper. With a bit of careful wriggling and nibbling, they'd make a perfect pair of ear plugs. I doubted they'd work for Mrs Wilson, but they

were good enough for me. Let the guinea pigs party the night away. I'd be catching up on my beauty sleep!

CHAPTER SEVEN

Bunny Boot Camp

It had been a few days since we'd seen anything of our other neighbour, Madame Belladonna. EE joked that maybe she'd gone chasing chickens, but I thought I'd caught a glimpse of goggle-covered eyes watching me over the fence as I'd raced around the garden.

There was something very odd about her and I didn't just mean those crazy clothes. Even Mrs Wilson admitted to being curious.

'There's no Mr Belladonna, is there?' she asked as the family tucked into their dinner and I chomped on a carrot nearby. 'Only I'm sure I saw a man's face at the window when I knocked on her door this morning to ask if she wanted to come to *Superpets* with us. I wonder who it could have been?'

'I haven't seen any men going in there,' EE said. 'But we don't know much about her. Maybe she has a son?'

'Pretty Polly, Pretty Polly,' Lily chirped.

Mrs Wilson frowned. 'No, Lily, it was definitely a man. I think he might have had a moustache.'

'Perhaps we should get him a ticket, too,' EE said, rubbing his chin.

'Madame Belladonna said she can't come to the *Summer Special*,' Mrs Wilson replied. 'In fact, she went a bit strange when I mentioned it.'

EE smiled. 'Stranger than usual, you mean?'

Nodding, Mrs Wilson said, 'Yes, she let out this high-pitched squawking laugh and said "I 'ope to be far, far away by zen."' She shrugged. 'She must be going on holiday. Maybe the man

is looking after the house while she's away.'

I didn't know who the mystery man was or where Madame Belladonna was going, but it made me even more curious about our funny neighbour. As soon as my big *Superpets* race was over, I planned to do a bit of investigating in next-door's garden.

☆ ☆ ☆

EE was turning into an army sergeant about my training. No matter how fast I zoomed around our homemade obstacle course, he wasn't happy.

'You can do better than that, Harriet!' he bellowed, eyebrows beetling together

over the top of the stopwatch. 'We need to shave five seconds off that time or Taz is going to stamp all over you. They don't call him the Tabby Tornado for nothing!'

Puffing and panting, I scowled up at him. It was all right for him! No one was expecting him to become the world's first agility bunny. In fact, looking up at his tubby tummy, I didn't think anyone would be asking him to run around anything.

'There's no need to yell, Dad,' Susie said, fanning my hot ears with her clipboard. 'Harriet's a Stunt Bunny, not a racer.'

'Hmmmm,' EE said, not looking convinced. 'We can't risk losing our place on *Superpets*. Harriet must win.'

Susie looked worried as EE stroked his chin thoughtfully. 'What we need

is a Bunny Boot Camp,' he went on. 'And I know just the man to help.'

Minutes later, he was on the phone and it didn't take long for me to work out he was talking to our vet.

'Strict diet of hay and water, you say?' I heard him say and he poked his head around the kitchen door to study me. 'No treats at all? Sounds good to me.'

Huh. It might sound good to EE, but he wasn't the one eating it. Susie and I looked at each other and a nasty feeling crept over me. The vet and I didn't really get along. There'd been a silly misunderstanding once with a Labrador puppy in his surgery and the

vet had never forgotten it. I was sure he'd be keen to get his own back if he could.

EE was nodding importantly into the phone. 'Quite right,' he said. 'It does make sense for you to pop in here. We'll see you in the morning for a full check-up.'

I didn't like the sound of that at all. Normally when I saw the vet, horrible things involving needles happened. I was getting a bad feeling about EE's Bunny Boot Camp.

It didn't start well. I'm not really a morning person and the vet arrived

at the Wilson house before EE had even left for work. Under Susie's watchful eye, he took my temperature, shone his tiny torch into my eyes, weighed me and even checked my teeth. Finally he folded his arms in satisfaction.

'This rabbit is in perfect health. There's really no need to put her on a diet.'

Chewing on his fingernail, EE said, 'That's all very well, but is she fit enough to win the race?'

Our vet chuckled and shook his head. 'Be sensible, Mr Wilson. Rabbits aren't made for agility racing. It's the most ridiculous thing I ever heard.'

EE frowned. 'Ordinary bunnies maybe,

but Harriet is rather unusual.'

With a shudder, the vet glared at me. 'I know. It took us three days to clean up the surgery last time she came to see us.'

Was he still going on about that? Anyone would think it was my fault

the computer blew up. Honestly, some people could really hold a grudge.

'She didn't mean to do it,' Susie said, lifting me up and cuddling me. 'And I think she can beat Taz. Harriet is a super-bunny.'

The vet laughed as though she'd told him a funny joke and picked up his bag to leave. 'If that rabbit wins the race, I'll eat my stethoscope.'

Now that was something I wouldn't mind seeing and it looked as though EE felt the same way. Once he'd shown the vet out, he came back with a determined expression on his face. 'Well, Harriet, ready for Bunny Boot Camp?'

I sat up on my back legs and waggled my paws. Whatever it took to beat Tornado Taz, I'd do it. Rabbit Racer was ready to run!

CHAPTER EIGHT

Salt and Pepper Shake Things Up

He might not be about to win any races himself, but, when it came to running a boot camp, EE was no slouch. Armed with a clipboard, I spent each sunrise sprinting laps around the garden and doing bunny-kick press-ups. Lunch was a carrot and cabbage smoothie served

by Susie's mum and snacks were off the menu, in spite of Lily's best efforts to feed me Smudge's biscuits. At sunset, I practised my rabbit punches on Susie's gloved hands and panted up and down the garden steps while EE glared at the stopwatch, frowning. Smudge watched lazily from his usual spot on top of the guinea pig hutch and pretended he wasn't interested in whether I won or lost. I knew he was rooting for me really, even if he did sometimes wish he could be more like Tornado Taz.

By the time the night before the race arrived, I was fighting fit. Even EE seemed satisfied.

'Great work, Harriet!' he cried as I finished my final run up the steps and tried to catch my breath. 'All you need now is a good night's sleep and you'll be ready for anything Taz can throw at you.'

Huh, I thought, there's no chance of that happening, not with those giggling guinea pigs around. But even Salt and Pepper seemed to understand that something important was happening and were quiet as we settled down for the night. I wasn't taking any chances, though; I had my carrot-top ear plugs handy just in case the guinea pigs changed their minds.

I was woken up by a loud rustling noise outside my hutch. The garden was dark, clouds covering the moon. Salt and Pepper were silent. Hopping forwards, I peered out, wondering whether Smudge had popped outside

for a midnight snack. When the clouds parted, I was puzzled to see the moonlight flash on something shiny outside my door. Then a scarf-covered face loomed in front of me and I became even more confused. It looked like Madame Belladonna, but what on earth was she doing out at this time of night? And why was she in our garden?

'We meet again, 'Arriet 'Oudini,' she whispered, holding up a pair of bolt cutters.

I shook my head to dislodge my ear plugs. Madame Belladonna's voice sounded funny, deeper than usual and

strangely familiar. If I didn't know better, I'd say she almost sounded like a man. She snapped off the padlocks on my door and reached inside.

'We go on ze leetle journey,' she murmured as she lifted me out of my hutch.

I wriggled and struggled, but Madame Belladonna was surprisingly strong. Before I knew it, she'd pushed me into the round birdcage we'd seen her carrying in on the day she'd first arrived, through the open bottom. She clipped the bottom of the cage back on, trapping me inside. In a flash, I knew Lily had been wrong; it had

never been ‘Pretty Polly’s’ house. It was mine!

There wasn’t much room inside. My tail was squashed against the wire bars at the back and my whiskers poked out of the sides. Over my head, a little swing banged against my ears and a tiny bell tinkled when I moved. Madame Belladonna picked the cage up and held me level with her nose.

'Say ze goodbyes to your old life, 'Arriet. You're my bunny now!'

If I hadn't understood what was happening before, I did now. Madame Belladonna was more than just the little old lady who lived next door – she was a rabbit-napper and I was the target of her evil plans. I didn't know where or why she was taking me, but I had no intention of going anywhere. It was time for a Stunt-Bunny style escape. But how? The cage was small and I had no room to kick my legs.

Madame Belladonna turned round and headed towards the fence between our garden and hers. The cage swung

round and I saw my comfy hutch disappearing behind me. My eyes strayed to the guinea pigs' run. If I could wake Salt and Pepper up, maybe they could raise the alarm. Furiously, I waggled my ears backwards and forwards. The bell on the swing jangled and chimed. In the guinea pig hutch, a faint rustling began in the straw. Peering out of the cage, I saw the flash of black eyes at the bars and I wriggled even more.

Suddenly, the air was filled with high-pitched meeping as Salt and Pepper realised what was happening. They raced around their hutch, thudding

into the walls and crashing into the door. Madame Belladonna muttered under her breath and speeded up. The birdcage jerked around, making the bell tinkle even more. Crossing my paws, I hoped all the noise was enough to wake the Wilsons up.

Madame Belladonna was just about to swing me and the birdcage over the fence when EE flung the bedroom window open.

'What is going on out there?' he bellowed. 'Some of us are trying to get some sleep!'

Madam Belladonna froze and the birdcage spun round, giving me a

rollercoaster view of EE's frowning face and the guinea pigs' wriggling noses. For one horrible moment, I thought EE wouldn't spot me in the dark, but the bell above my head continued to ring, giving the game away.

'Stop right there, whoever you are, or I'll call the police!' he yelled. 'Hang on, Harriet, I'm coming down!'

'Time for ze quick getaway!' Madame Belladonna muttered and she lifted her leg to climb into her garden. Heart pounding, I willed EE to hurry. In a few seconds I'd be over the fence and EE wouldn't know where I'd gone. I had to do something to stall my kidnapper!

CHAPTER NINE

Not So Bella Donna

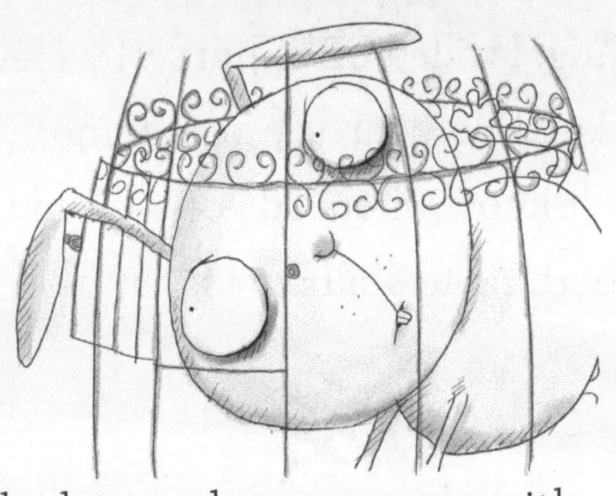

I had seconds to come up with a plan. Desperately, I stared around the birdcage. The bell was still ringing madly and the swing was – well – swinging, but they were no use to me now. The door was bird-sized; I'd be lucky to fit my paw through it.

I needed another escape route, fast!

Madame Belladonna had one leg straddling the fence and was balancing on top, ready to swing me and her other leg over. She wobbled and the cage trembled with her. Suddenly, I knew what to do. If I could make Madame Belladonna lose her balance, she'd have to let go of me and the cage would fall to the ground. She wouldn't have time to come back and get me before EE made it to the garden.

Wriggling as much as I could, I pushed my tail up the cage wall and balanced on my front legs, in a rabbit paw-stand. Then, with an enormous thrust, I kicked

my legs towards the dome at the top of the cage.

'Stop eet!' Madame Belladonna shouted, clasping her bobble hat to her head with her free hand and glaring at me. 'We will fall to ze death if you are not careful!'

I kicked out again, even harder this time. At the same time, the back door of the Wilson house flew open and EE appeared in his tartan dressing gown and football-shaped slippers, with Susie and the rest of the family close behind.

'Halt! Who goes there?'

It was all too much for Madame Belladonna. She lost her balance and

began to slide sideways. I fired my hardest kick yet at the top of the cage and the handle slipped from her fingers. With a startled yell, Madame Belladonna fell into her garden, just as the cage crashed to the ground and broke apart.

For a second, I lay there, breathing hard. Then I heard a scrabbling noise next door and I knew Madame Belladonna was getting away. Well, I wasn't having that – no one tries to bunny-nap me and escape so easily! Without thinking, I was up and racing towards the beach-ball at the bottom of the garden. Leaping on to it, I bounced

high into the air. A quick glance down told me that Madame Belladonna was running towards her house with surprising speed for an old lady. So she thought she could escape a rabbit racer, did she? We'd just see about that!

Changing course mid-air, I aimed for her bobble hat. I'd never had to land

on a moving target before and it took all my Stunt Bunny skills to do it. Madame Belladonna let out a terrified yell.

'Aaaargh! Get off, you crazy animal!'

She shook her head from side to side. The hat began to come loose and the scarf fell down to her chin. I gripped on and felt myself sliding forwards over

her nose. As I came face to face with her, I was in for a shock. Underneath the hat and scarf, she had thick, curly hair and a big, black moustache. Madame Belladonna wasn't a Madame at all. She was a *he*! Our next-door neighbour was none other than my old enemy, the Great Maldini!

He reached up and grabbed me. 'I 'ave you now, 'Arriet 'Oudini. Soon we will be far from 'ere and you will be ze new star of my magic show!'

Not if I had anything to do with it. Remembering my Bunny Boot Camp boxing sessions with Susie, I lifted both paws and delivered a flurry of

rabbit punches to the Great Maldini's long, pointy nose.

'Ouch, by dose!' he yelled, letting go of me to clutch at his face.

In a flash, I scrambled up on to his head and kicked off hard, aiming for the tree branch above. All that agility training came in handy as my claws gripped the bark. I picked my way carefully along the thin branch until I was over the Wilsons' garden. Then I threw myself upwards into a triple bunny backflip and landed in Susie's waiting arms.

'Oh, Harriet,' Susie sobbed, burying her face in my grey fur. 'You were ever so brave.'

EE waved a garden fork over the fence as the Great Maldini vanished into the house. Seconds later, we heard the roar of an engine. Rushing to the front garden, we were just in time to see the Great Maldini burst through his front door on a shiny red motorbike.

He revved the engine and raised a hand as he sped off down the street. 'Until we meet again, 'Arriet 'Oudini! Ze Great Maldini never gives up!'

Lights came on in all the other houses as people came out to see what the

hubbub was about. The Wilson family stared at the disappearing motorbike in disbelief.

'So the Great Maldini is Madame Belladonna's son?' Mrs Wilson said in a confused voice, as Lily snuggled sleepily against her shoulder.

EE waved away the last of the smoke from the motorbike's engine. 'I don't think our neighbour was who she said

she was. I suspect Madame Belladonna was the Great Maldini all along!'

Susie gasped and held me tightly. 'And he was after Harriet again, but she was too clever for him.'

Smiling, EE looked at me. 'She was. Salt and Pepper helped too. If they hadn't made so much noise, we might not have woken up.'

Then Mrs Wilson glanced at her watch. 'Goodness me, back to bed, everyone,' she commanded. 'It's Harriet's big race in a few hours and I think we've had quite enough excitement for one night.'

'But what if the Great Maldini comes back?" Susie said, a worried expression

on her face. 'Harriet could still be in danger.'

EE thought for a moment. 'I suppose she could sleep indoors for once.'

Smudge didn't look pleased, but I twitched my nose happily. Salt and Pepper were bound to be excited from all the adventures, so I doubted I'd get any sleep at all next to them. No, a nice cosy snooze in the warmth of my travel basket was exactly what I needed to be ready for *Superpets*. When I woke up, Taz was going to be in for the race of his life.

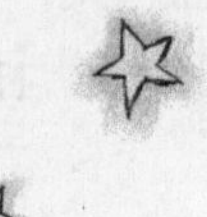

CHAPTER TEN

A Slippery Situation

The *Superpets* studio was packed for the special race show. Backstage, people were squeezed into every corner and most of them wore T-shirts with 'Team Taz' or 'Team Harriet' on them. Even Spike-tacular had special outfits on, each of them with a letter which spelled

out my name. Doodle and Miranda had clearly chosen their side and were wearing Taz T-shirts and little furry cat ears. Miranda was fussing around Tim, offering him chocolate fudge cake and cups of tea.

'I've always been a cat person,' she said, fluttering her eyelashes at him. 'And Doodle simply adores them.'

'I bet she does,' Tim replied, watching Doodle bare her teeth in an unfriendly grin at Taz. 'For breakfast or dinner, usually?'

Miranda threw back her head and laughed loudly. 'You're so funny, Tim. How have we got along without you?'

Gloria bustled up to them both. 'It's almost time for the race,' she said to Tim. 'I hope Taz is in tip-top form?'

Taz swished his tail and let out an enthusiastic *mrrrow*. Tim nodded. 'He's looking forward to it.'

Turning to EE and Susie, Gloria smiled. 'No need to ask if Harriet is ready. I bet she's raring to go.'

EE yawned. 'She's certainly been training hard.'

'Excellent,' Gloria said, rubbing her hands together. 'I'm hoping for a real ratings winner to knock that dancing show on the other channel off the top spot.'

As the other adults talked, Miranda rummaged in her handbag and offered a small white tube to Susie. 'I almost forgot to give you this. It's special cream to stop Harriet's paws from hurting. Make sure you rub it in before the race begins.' She lowered her voice. 'Don't tell anyone about this. I don't want Taz to get jealous.'

Susie took the tube and peered at it doubtfully. 'Thank you, Miranda. Are you sure it will help?'

Miranda gave a thin smile. 'Oh yes. It will definitely do the trick.'

Gloria checked her watch. 'Come along, racers. It's time we got you to the start line.'

By the time we reached the sawdust-filled ring where the race was taking place, Susie seemed more nervous than I was. 'Good luck, Harriet,' she said, squeezing the tube Miranda had given her and rubbing the cream into my paws with shaking hands. 'Be careful.'

I sniffed at my feet suspiciously. It wasn't like Miranda to be helpful and whatever was in that cream, it smelled

strange. Beside us, Tim was whispering last-minute instructions into Taz's twitching ear. Then he patted his head and both owners backed away. It was just the cat and me. Gloria hovered nearby, talking into the camera.

'It's a world exclusive! *Superpets* favourite, Harriet Houdini, races against newcomer, Tornado Taz.' She leaned into the camera, a tense look on her face. 'Stay tuned to find out who wins!'

I glanced over at Taz. He was poised at the start line, his ears flat and his tail wrapped with a special support bandage. Hopping towards him, I gave him a 'may-the-best-pet-win' nudge

and he turned his green-eyed gaze on me. Without blinking, he reached down and touched his nose to mine. Then he turned away and I took up my place on the starting line once more.

Gloria was looking our way and she had a tiny starter's gun in her hand. 'Superpets, are you ready?'

I glanced out at the two identical obstacle courses side by side. Was that a see-saw at the start? Susie and I hadn't practised with one of those. But EE had shown me some clips of dog agility races and I'd seen the best way to handle a see-saw. I hoped it was as easy as it looked.

'On your marks . . . get set . . .' Gloria aimed the pistol up in the air and squeezed the trigger. 'Go!'

And we were off. Up to the see-saw, we were pretty evenly matched. Taz hit the yellow slope ahead of me and I saw him slow down to wait for the end to drop before he crossed it. When I hit the plastic, something strange happened. Instead of slowing down the way I meant to, my paws didn't grip. They slid. So rather than crossing in a calm, controlled way, I zoomed up one side, then down the other, and hit the sawdust at the other side before Taz.

I didn't have time to wonder what had happened, though. The next obstacle, the weaving poles, was hurtling towards me. Taz and I bobbed from side to side almost in unison, the red-and-white sticks wobbling as we rounded them. Then we were through and

coming up to a jump. The criss-crossed bars looked very high. I snatched a deep breath and somersaulted over them.

A quick glance to my right told me Taz had cleared the jump too. Next up was a cloth tunnel, followed by another jump. We were neck and neck coming

up to the wall of the ring, where our paths split. As I peeled off to the left and Taz sped away to the right, I looked ahead. We had one more jump and the balance bar left to cover. If things carried on as they were, it looked like Taz was going to win.

But I wasn't ready to give up just yet and, gathering up all my strength, I pounded down the back straight and soared over the last jump. Over on the other side of the ring, I could see Taz swarming up the wooden plank which led to the red plastic balance beam. A second behind him, I zipped up my own plank. But once again,

my feet refused to grip the plastic. As Taz picked his way over and began his descent at the other end, I found myself sliding along the beam, gathering speed like a surfer on a wave.

I couldn't stop. Instead of going down the plank at the end as Taz had done, I flew off the plastic beam and overtook the cat in mid-air. In a flurry of sawdust, I landed ahead of him. Eyes fixed on the finish line, I scampered for it as fast as I could. Everything seemed to slow down. Taz was panting next to me. With one last surge of my back feet, I pushed forwards – and my nose nudged across the line just before his.

The crowd went wild. Susie was hugging me, Taz was licking me and Gloria was smiling from ear to ear.

'We have a winner!' she cried,

beaming into the camera. 'An unusual finish from Harriet, but it won her the race. Three cheers for Harriet Houdini – Rabbit Racer!'

CHAPTER ELEVEN

Pets-A-Go-Go

The show cut to an advert break straight after the race. All the other pets and their owners crowded around us, offering congratulations and clapping.

'Well done, Harriet!' Susie said, lifting me up and twirling around. 'You're the most amazing bunny I've ever seen.'

EE agreed. 'It was a brilliant race. But what on earth was all the sliding about? I'm sure we didn't practise that at home.'

I looked at my paws. They looked the same as always, except for a thin layer of shiny cream. Susie's hands flew to her mouth. 'I think it's my fault. Miranda gave me something to put on Harriet's feet. She said it would stop them from hurting.'

Everyone looked at Miranda, who went red. 'It's an old family recipe,' she declared. 'I had no idea it would make Harriet's paws slippery.'

EE took the tube of cream Susie was holding up. Carefully, he peeled back

the plain white label and peered at what was underneath. 'Beeswax furniture polish,' he read. 'To make your surfaces super shiny.'

Gloria frowned at Miranda. 'I find it hard to believe that you didn't realise this would affect Harriet's race,' she said in a stern voice. 'In fact, I think you knew exactly what would happen.'

Miranda didn't say anything. She stood there with Doodle at her feet, glowering at everyone.

The cameraman waved a panicky hand at Gloria. 'Back on in ten seconds.'

'Places, everyone,' Gloria commanded. 'We'll sort this out later.'

The other pets and their owners scattered to various positions on the stage, leaving Gloria centre-stage.

'Welcome back.' Gloria smiled into the camera, as though nothing was wrong. 'Wow, what an opening to the show that was! But the surprises don't stop there. Here on *Superpets*, we like to shake things up. Each of our talented animals has been working on a secret new trick for this *Summer Special*, hoping to amaze you. Let's start by meeting the Tap Hogs!'

The camera cut to Spike-tacular, who launched straight into a noisy tap-dancing number. Once they'd finished,

Cherry bamboozled everyone with her new card trick, the terrapins wowed the crowd with their high-dive act and Lulu the chimpanzee made them gasp with her flaming hula hoop routine. I was impressed – everyone had been working really hard! After each pet's performance, Doodle and Miranda grew paler and paler and when the camera swung round to them, I saw Doodle gulp. This was going to be interesting.

Gloria clapped her hands. 'Now it's time for our final act. Doodle the opera-singing Poodle will attempt to shatter glass using her voice alone!'

The stage lights dimmed and a spotlight glared down on Doodle and a single crystal goblet on a table next to her. The audience was hushed. Looking nervous, the poodle opened her mouth and began to howl. As her voice got higher and higher, I saw people in the crowd jamming their fingers in their ears. Spike-tacular rolled themselves into spiny balls,

Gloria looked strained and I wrapped my ears around my head. After two minutes of woeful warbling, the glass showed no sign of shattering and Doodle had gone a funny pink colour. Then Miranda stepped forwards and stood beside the table.

'Goodness me, what's that?' she called, pointing high above the audience. Everyone looked up and even the cameramen spun their cameras around, but there was nothing to see. Seconds later, we heard a loud crash on stage, followed by the tinkling of broken glass. When we all turned back to look at Doodle, the table was empty

and Miranda was looking smug.

'Oh dear, you missed Doodle's amazing trick,' she said, in a sickly sweet voice. 'Never mind!'

Gloria looked disappointed and disapproving at the same time. 'That's a shame,' she said. 'But – er – sadly we don't have time for a repeat performance because now it's crunch-time for one of these pets. The animal whose new trick failed to wow the crowd will be leaving *Superpets* for good!'

There was a gasp as Gloria's words sank in. Then the stage lights dimmed and a spotlight began to bounce around the pets, settling on each one for a few

seconds before landing on another. Dramatic music began to play in the background. Sam and Spike-tacular looked nervous and I thought Trevor might faint, squashing his terrapins in the process. Cherry was busily counting, as usual, and Lulu was whirling her hula hoop in a worried way. Miranda

didn't look anxious at all, though; both her and Doodle had their snooty noses high in the air.

The spotlight moved faster as the music grew louder. Then, with a final crash of drums, it settled on the big, curly hair-dos of Doodle and Miranda. Gloria turned to the spectators smoothly.

'Let's have a big round of applause for Doodle the opera-singing Poodle and her owner, Miranda!' She fired a brisk smile towards the spotlit pair. 'I'm sure we've all enjoyed having them on the show, but all good things must come to an end.'

Miranda and Doodle scowled furiously in her direction and I thought Miranda would argue. Then she seemed to remember that the cameras were rolling and nodded at Doodle. Teeth fixed in a forced grin, the pair waved to the cheering crowd.

As Gloria signed off, Miranda leaned down to me. 'You haven't seen the last of us, Harriet Houdini,' she hissed

through her smile. 'We'll be back, and when we are, you'd better watch out.'

Doodle lunged for me, jaws snapping, but Taz leaped in between us. Spitting, he lashed out a paw and hit Doodle square on the nose. Doodle yelped and backed off, her own paw holding her face.

Tim saw and patted his cat on the head. 'It looks like you two are firm friends,' he said, winking at me. 'I think Taz is going to enjoy being a Superpet!'

I looked at Taz and waggled my paws at him in thanks. Now that Miranda and Doodle were going, *Superpets* was going to be one hundred percent fun.

But I decided I'd leave the racing to Taz in future. Being a Stunt Bunny was more than enough excitement for me!

1st
SB' RACING
SB
the End
XSB

Acknowledgements

Big smoochy kisses to my husband, Lee, and daughter, Tania, for being brilliant in every way. Huge thanks to Superstar Agent, Jo Williamson, for being my very own Number 1 Fan (minus the bunny ears), to Richard and Janice Slater (in-laws extraordinaire) and to the Simon and Schuster A-Listers: Venetia, Editor Jane, Designer Jane, Phil and every single fabulous person who helped make this book happen. Harriet says the carrot juice is on her!

SHOWBIZ SENSATION

BACK BY POPULAR DEMAND

Winner of 4 Bunnies!

Now read STUNT BUNNY'S first adventure, SHOWBIZ SENSATION!

THE NATION'S SWEETHEART!

Harriet Houdini is just settling in to life with her new family, when she is spotted by the producer of the hit TV show *Superpets* and starts her showbiz career.

From daring bunny-backflips to thrilling escapes Harriet is a true Stunt Bunny – but does she have what it takes to become a Superpet?

978-1-84738-727-1
£4.99

TOUR TROUBLES

SOLD OUT

With special guests Spike-tacular!

Harriet Houdini: Stunt Bunny is back, as the star of *Superpets Live!*

With visions of posh hotels, adoring fans and performing her famous bunny-backflips in front of live audiences, Harriet can't wait for the tour of *Superpets.* But evil Miranda plans to make singing poodle, Doodle, the headline act at any cost . . . Can Harriet's Stunt Bunny antics ensure she remains the star of the show?

* * * * *

978-1-84738-728-8
£4.99

NO.1 BUNNY!

COMING SOON
TO A BOOK STORE
NEAR YOU
STUNT BUNNY
MEDAL
MAYHEM

STUNT
BUNNY